PATRICIA SCARRY'S
Little Willy and Spike

The Adventures of a Rabbit and His Porcupine Friend

Illustrated by Lucinda McQueen

A GOLDEN BOOK • NEW YORK

Western Publishing Company, Inc. Racine, Wisconsin 53404

Contents

Captain Father Rabbit

Little Willy and Spike were walking toward the pond with Father Rabbit.

Father was going to teach them to row a boat.

"Daddy, do we have to wear these life jackets?" asked Little Willy.

"Yes. In case the boat tips over," said Father.

"How could it do that, Mr. Rabbit?" asked Spike.

"Oh, lots of ways. Especially if someone stands up," said Father. "Don't ever stand up in a boat."

"I feel silly in this life jacket," said Little Willy.

"What if someone sees us? I'd be embarrassed," said Spike.

"It is a rule of the sea: young people wear life jackets on boats," said Father.

"And never stand up in a boat!" chimed in the two friends.

"Correct!" said Father Rabbit.

They reached the pond. There was the little boat.

"You can haul her in with the rope," said Father.

Little Willy and Spike pulled the boat to shore and jumped in.

"Be sure to stay in the middle. We don't want the boat to tip over," called Father Rabbit.

He untied the rope and jumped neatly into the middle of the boat.

"Whew! It's tippety!" cried Little Willy.

"That's why we can't stand up in it," said Spike, looking hard at Mr. Rabbit, who was standing up in the stern.

Mr. Rabbit quickly sat down.

"Can we begin rowing now, Daddy?" asked Little Willy,
holding on to an oar.

"First I'll explain," said Father Rabbit. "When I say 'Dip,'
you dip your oars in the water. When I say 'Pull,' you pull your oars
through the water. Then 'Out' means take your oars out of the water.
Dip, pull, and out."

Little Willy and Spike learned fast. It was fun. With every
stroke of their oars the boat moved forward.

Suddenly there was a *bump!* And an *ouch!*

Poor Spike landed in the bottom of the rowboat.

"You pulled your oar through the air, Spike, not the water,"
said Father Rabbit. And he chuckled.

Spike scrambled up from the bottom of the boat.

"Don't stand up!" cried Father Rabbit.

"No, sir!" answered Spike. And he sat down, fast, on the seat.

"You are learning very well," said Father. "Now we'll do it
again. Dip! Pu-u-u-ll! And out!"

"My life jacket is too tight, Daddy. I'm going to loosen it a bit," said Little Willy. He stood up to loosen the string....

"Never stand up in a boat!" shouted Father and Spike.

Little Willy plunked down quickly. He looked embarrassed.

"I forgot," he said.

So Father Rabbit began chanting again, "Dip. Pull. Out!"

They skimmed along the water quickly. Everyone felt so proud.

"Wait a minute," said Father Rabbit. "I just need that cushion in back of you."

He stood up in the boat, and...

Splash! Over it went!

Everybody fell into the water. Down, down they went, where everything was blue and green and wet.

Then up, up they came to the surface of the pond. And all around them everything was floating on top of the water. Oars. Cushions. Paper cups. All sorts of things you would never imagine could swim.

"Oh, Daddy. Shame on you!" laughed Little Willy.

"Mr. Rabbit, don't you know you should never, ever stand up in a boat?" howled Spike. He squealed with laughter.

Father Rabbit didn't even apologize. He just hung on to the boat and said, "Aren't you glad I made you wear your life jackets? Ho! Ho! Ho!"

The Hiding Place

First the big comfy chair in Little Willy's house was covered with pink-and-white cloth.

Then Mother Rabbit knitted Little Willy a sweater of pink-and-white wool.

One day Mother made a batch of cookies. She asked Little Willy what color he'd like the icing to be.

"*Pink!*" he said. "Pink icing is my favorite."

He helped his mother frost the cookies. Then he took a cookie in each paw, and, wearing his pink-and-white sweater, he ran to sit in the pink-and-white comfy chair and eat the cookies.

You could hardly see Little Willy at all!

"Where are you?" called Mother Rabbit.

"I'm here!" cried Little Willy.

But she couldn't see him.

"Where?" she asked.

"Here, Mommy!" And he laughed.

"Where is here?" called his mother. "Under the table? Beside the window? Under the chair?"

"You're getting close," laughed Little Willy.

"Tell me, where are you? I can't see you!" called Mother.

"You'll see me in a minute," he answered.

Little Willy ate the last bite of his second cookie. Then he jumped off the pink-and-white chair and ran across the kitchen.

"Here I am!" he cried.

His mother reached out and caught him.

"You've been hiding," she said.

"I've been here all the time," he said.

He liked to tease her.

"Next time I'm going to make *chocolate* cookies. Then I'll be able to see you!" said Mother Rabbit.

It was a little game they liked to play.

13

Bringing Home
The Groceries

Mother Rabbit was making her grocery list.

"Mother, let me go to the store for you," said Little Willy.

"It's a long way to carry a bag of groceries," Mother said.

"But I would like to," said Little Willy.

He took the shopping list from his mother and put the money in his pocket. Then off he went to Mr. Charlie Pig's store.

He handed Mr. Pig his mother's list.

Little Willy sniffed in the wonderful smells of raisins and chocolate and tea that mingled in the little store. Mr. Charlie Pig got the things that were on the list.

"Two apples for Mrs. Rabbit. Two bananas. A box of cookies.

14

A jar of mustard. And here is a lollipop for you," Mr. Pig said. He tucked the leftover money into Little Willy's pocket. Then he handed him the grocery bag.

"Now, I hope this grocery bag won't be too heavy for you," he said.

"Oh, no," said Little Willy.

Oh! It did seem a bit heavy.

"Good-by, Mr. Pig," called Little Willy.

And he set off for home with the groceries.

He carried the grocery bag in his arms. It was too heavy. He tried dragging it.

Then he saw a friendly-looking rock. He set the bag down on the grass and took a lick of his lollipop.

Mmm, it was good!

After a while he picked up the grocery bag. *Oof!* The bottom of the bag was wet. So he held it by the bottom. He didn't see the mustard jar fall out as he staggered on his way.

Little Willy thought he must have carried that bag a mile. Then suddenly he remembered the money Mr. Charlie Pig had put in his pocket. Which pocket?

He sat down on the grass and dug into both pockets.

Oh, no! The money was gone. Mr. Pig had put it in the pocket with the hole.

Little Willy felt so gloomy that he opened the package of cookies and ate four of them. They were chocolate-chip. So he ate one more. And he felt better. He got up and started walking again.

Someone was calling him.

"Little Willy, stop! It's me!" cried Spike, running after him. "Look what I found," he said. "Two bananas! You can have one."

"Thank you, Spike. They're mine," said Little Willy.

The two friends sat down and munched on the bananas.

"There is a hole in your grocery bag," said Spike.

"I know. But now it will be lighter," said Little Willy.

"And I found some money. Look!" said Spike.

"That's mine, too," said Little Willy. He stuffed it into his good pocket.

"I found this jar of mustard, too, and an apple," said Spike.

The two friends set out for home. Now and then they stopped. So it was only natural that they bit into the apples. Soon the cookies were eaten. Before long, only the mustard was left.

Mrs. Rabbit was waiting at the door for the groceries.

She held up the money and the mustard.

"Whatever happened to the other things?" she asked.

Little Willy explained about the hole in the bag.

"Now you'll never let me fetch the groceries for you again," he sighed.

"Oh, yes, I will," said Mother. "I will ask you to go tomorrow. But I think Spike should go with you to help. I need some apples, some bananas, and some cookies!"

And everybody laughed.

17

The Ladybug

"Little Willy, you are going to have good luck. There is a ladybug sitting on your shoulder!" cried Spike.

"Oh!" Little Willy turned to look.

"Don't touch her! You'll scare her away!" said Spike. "Leave her and she'll bring you good luck."

"How?" asked Little Willy.

"Something nice will happen," said Spike. "But you have to sit still."

"Even if my leg is falling asleep?" asked Little Willy.

"Oh, I can see that you don't believe in ladybugs. Come on. We'll ask your mother if I'm right," said Spike.

Little Willy got to his feet carefully. He didn't want to upset the ladybug. He was so busy trying to see her that he didn't see the wagon on the path.

He tripped over it.

Crash!

"*Ouch!*" howled Little Willy. "I've hurt my leg."

"It's all right. The ladybug is still on your shoulder," called Spike. "She wants to bring you good luck."

Little Willy limped on one foot.

"The ladybug would like you to be more careful and look where you're going," said Spike.

"I will try. I can't wait for my good luck to happen," said Little Willy.

He limped down the path behind Spike, who kept his eye on the ladybug.

"She's still there," whispered Spike, when...

Bang!

They bumped into the wheelbarrow! It was filled with firewood that tumbled out.

"Oh, my elbow hurts!" wailed Little Willy.

"Ouch! My head! Ouch! Ouch!" groaned Spike. "But the ladybug is still on your shoulder. She's going to bring you good luck."

"So far I've fallen and hurt myself twice since I met this ladybug," said Little Willy.

"I think you are lucky that this ladybug is still with you after all that's happened," said Spike.

"We're almost at the house now," said Little Willy. He limped along carefully and rubbed his elbow.

Spike turned around to look at the ladybug, and...

Splash!

Down they went, into a huge tub of water.

"Oooh, Mother must have left the washtub here," gasped Little Willy.

They were both soaking wet, and laughing.

"Oh, look, Little Willy. Your ladybug is floating in the water!" cried Spike.

"We will rescue her," said Little Willy.

He hobbled on his good foot until he found a leaf. In a minute, the ladybug was sitting safely on it.

"She doesn't look upset at all," said Spike.

Just then the screen door flew open. Mother Rabbit said, "Oh, you've found a ladybug. That brings good luck, you know."

"So far she's brought me a sore foot and a bumped elbow. And we're both dripping wet," said Little Willy. He and Spike burst out laughing again.

Just then, the ladybug flew off her leaf and away.

"She's going home to her children," said Mother.

"I wonder when she'll bring me good luck," said Little Willy.

"Right now. I can smell it in the kitchen!" cried Spike, grinning.

They followed their noses, and on the table they found a big, fresh cake covered with chocolate icing.

"M*mmm*, I couldn't think of any better luck than eating my own mother's chocolate cake!" said Little Willy.

"Now do you believe that ladybugs bring good luck?" asked Spike.

"I do," replied Little Willy, through a mouthful of chocolate cake.

Businessmen

"Mother, how can we earn some money?" asked Little Willy.

"Oh, there are lots of ways. You and Spike could wash the windows," said Mother.

The two friends were silent.

"You could weed the garden," said Mother.

More silence.

"Or you could sell lemonade," she said.

"Sell lemonade? Oh, boy!" said Little Willy.

"We could make lots of money doing that," said Spike.

So Mother Rabbit helped them a little. Soon they were standing in the lane, beside a sign they had made. It said:

"COLD LEMONADE. TWO CENTS A CUP."

"Good luck!" called Mr. and Mrs. Rabbit as they went off to pick blackberries.

Little Willy and Spike stood by their lemonade stand waiting to grow rich.

Old Mr. Badger came by, looking hot and tired.

"Would you like a cup of lemonade, Mr. Badger?" asked Little Willy.

"Why, that would be very nice," said Mr. Badger. He was so nearsighted that he didn't see the sign.

He enjoyed a cold glass of lemonade. And another. Then he thanked his young friends and went on his way.

"I just couldn't tell him it cost two pennies a cup," said Little Willy.

"Neither could I," said Spike. "He's so nice."

COLD
LEMONADE
TWO CENTS
A CUP

Then down the lane came the five little hedgehogs.

Yes. They certainly would like some lemonade. They each drank a cup, thirstily. They called out, "Thank you!" and went away home.

"What happened?" demanded Spike. "They didn't pay!" he cried, amazed.

"I think they are too little to read the sign," said Little Willy.

Oh, dear. The two businessmen were growing discouraged. Now no one came by for a long, long time.

Then, at last, Mrs. Duck arrived with her children.

"I will buy a cup for each of the ducklings," she said.

Aha! Little Willy and Spike quickly filled five paper cups for the little ducks.

Mrs. Duck felt in her purse for the money. She dug. And she dug again. Then she said, "I am so embarrassed. I seem to have spent every penny at the market. But I won't forget that I owe you. I promise!"

And she herded her ducklings down the lane.

Poor Little Willy and Spike were discouraged. They were ready to go home penniless. But just then Mr. and Mrs. Rabbit returned with their blackberries.

"Well, did you make some money?" asked Father.

The two businessmen were ready to cry.

"We've given away a lot of lemonade," said Spike.

"Well, I'll buy a cup for myself and one for your mother," said Father Rabbit.

"Yes, *sir!*" said Little Willy, grinning.

"Mmmm, that was so good that I'd like another," said Mother.

"Yes, two more cupfuls of lemonade, please," said Father.

They were very thirsty from picking blackberries.

"Delicious," said Father. "Now I'd like to buy a cup for each of you."

"Oh, we couldn't do that," said Spike. "After all, they are your lemons."

Father firmly placed four more pennies on the table.

"Drink up!" he said.

"Thank you," said Little Willy and Spike. And even though they could barely stand the sight of lemonade, they drank it down.

"Business is improving," said Mother.

Just then, one of the ducklings waddled down the lane and dropped ten pennies on the table.

"Mommy said I was to pay you," he quacked.

"Oh, boy! Now we have some money!" cheered Little Willy and Spike.

And just as soon as they'd put the stand away, they ran all the way to Mr. Charlie Pig's store.

They each bought a paper glider with the money they'd earned. And they sailed them, up on the hill, all that lazy afternoon.

Happy Father's Day

It was Father's Day.

Little Willy and Spike were helping Mother make a special dessert for supper. They were tasting.

"What are you going to give Daddy for Father's Day, Little Willy?" asked Mother Rabbit.

"I think I will buy him a necktie," Little Willy said. And he ran to find his bank. He shook it. Only three pennies fell out.

"Oh, I don't think that will be enough money," said Mother.

Little Willy looked sad.

"It's much nicer to give a present that you've made yourself," said Mother.

Then she showed him the handsome pair of socks she'd knitted for Daddy.

"I'm going to make my father some fudge!" announced Spike.

"My father doesn't like fudge," said Little Willy.

"Then make him something that he needs," said Mother.

A short while later, Mother Rabbit heard loud hammering coming from her bedroom. She opened the door.

Oh, no! Little Willy and Spike had taken everything out of Father's closet. They were hammering long nails into the door.

"We're making a tie rack to hang his ties on," said Spike. "It was my idea."

"No, no. Those nails are dangerous. You must pull them out and put everything back in the closet," said Mother, beginning to pick up clothes from the floor.

Some time later she peeked into Little Willy's room.

"Stop!" she cried.

The two friends were gluing wooden blocks together. The glue was sticking to the rug, and to lots of other things.

"We are making bookends to hold Daddy's books together," said Little Willy.

"But he already has bookends," said Mother.

28

"Oh, what can I make him for Father's Day?" wailed Little Willy.

"You will think of something nice," said Mother.

She pulled a fuzzy block off the sticky carpet.

Spike ran home to make fudge. And Little Willy closed his door. He had to think.

He was quiet for such a long time that Mother Rabbit grew nervous. She peeked into his room again.

Little Willy was working with a big piece of paper. Mother closed the door softly.

After a while Little Willy brought her the present he had made for his father.

"Oh, he will love that," said Mother.

Together they wrapped the present in pretty paper and waited for Father to come home.

The special Father's Day dinner was delicious! Especially dessert. Father loved the socks that Mother had knitted for him.

He loved the box of candy that was just for him.

Then he opened Little Willy's present. And oh, how he smiled. He grinned!

It was a drawing of Father Rabbit.

"Little Willy, did you draw this picture by yourself? It looks just like me! It's *beautiful!*" he cried.

Father was so excited that he tacked the picture to the wall, right beside the table.

"Tomorrow we will put it in a gold frame," he said.

That made Little Willy so happy.

The Scarecrow

"Just look at all those crows eating our corn seed," said Father Rabbit.

"Now we won't have any corn on the cob to eat," said Little Willy.

"You need to make a scarecrow, Mr. Rabbit," said Spike.

"You are right, Spike, but I haven't the time," said Father. And he went off to work.

"What is a scarecrow?" asked Little Willy.

"It's a man you make out of straw. You dress him up in old clothes, then you put him in the field, and he scares the crows away," said Spike.

"Oh, boy! Let's make one ourselves!" cried Little Willy.

"We'll surprise your father," said Spike.

It was fun. In the attic they found some old trousers of Father Rabbit's. And a shirt. And a funny old hat.

Then they took a pile of straw from the barn. Mother Rabbit gave them strong kitchen string. And they went to work.

31

It wasn't as easy as they'd thought. They spent all afternoon stuffing the arms and legs of Father's old clothes with straw. Then they tied them here and there with string.

For the scarecrow's face they used a white cloth.

"I think he should have a scary face. He has to frighten crows, you know," said Spike.

"But maybe he should have a friendly face, because he is going to be in the field every day, helping us," said Little Willy.

It was hard to decide.

"Well, I'm going to paint his eyes a little bit scary," said Spike.

"But his mouth will be friendly," said Little Willy. And he waited for his turn to paint.

Even though he painted the mouth very carefully, the paint dripped down a bit.

"Oooh, after all my hard work, he looks cross!" groaned Little Willy, disappointed.

"Never mind, let's put him into the field before your father comes home," said Spike.

They had a hard time making the straw man stand up. But he did at last. As they worked, a strong wind came up.

"He's really scary, isn't he?" asked Spike.

"Yes, he's kind of spooky," said Little Willy.

"It's the way his sleeves flap in the wind," said Spike. "Flap! Flap! Flap!" And they both shuddered.

"He looks real!" squeaked Little Willy.

"He scares *me*!" cried Spike. And he began running for the house.

"Wait! Don't leave me here alone!" cried Little Willy.

They dashed into the house and slammed the front door. Then they crept up to the window. The scarecrow was shaking his arms wildly in the wind.

"I th-think he's walking this w-way," whispered Spike.

The two of them knelt by the window and shivered with fright. And that is how Father Rabbit found them.

He laughed and laughed.

"So, you made a scarecrow who scared *you!*" he said.

"I think it's his face, Daddy. He has a very scary face," said Little Willy.

"He is *supposed* to be scary," said Father. "But tonight his mean face will get washed off by the rain. And tomorrow you can make his face nice and friendly."

"We'll make him look kind," said Little Willy and Spike together.

"Not *too* kind. He's a wonderful scarecrow," said Father Rabbit. "He's scared some others besides yourselves."

"Who?"

"Who?"

"The crows! Look. There isn't a crow in sight!" said Father.

And there wasn't.

34

The Picnic

Little Willy was in the kitchen making sandwiches.

"One. Two. Three. Four. I have made four peanut butter sandwiches, Spike. Is that enough for our picnic?" he asked.

"Make two more, Little Willy. We may get really hungry," said Spike.

So Little Willy made two more.

Spike wrapped the sandwiches and put them on the table.

"Shall we take two pieces of cake?" asked Little Willy.

"Four pieces," said Spike.

Four pieces of chocolate cake were wrapped up and put on the table.

"Two apples?" asked Little Willy.

"Four," replied Spike. "We just might be starving."

Then Spike added a bag of cookies and a thermos of lemonade.

Now the picnic was piled high on the table.

"There's an awful lot to carry," said Spike.

"We'll share it," said Little Willy. "It's too bad that Owley can't come today. He has to help his mother."

Their knapsacks were lying empty on the floor.

"Oh, before we pack the picnic I want to put my paddleball into my sack," said Little Willy.

"And I'll get the pail and shovel. After all, we *are* going to the pond," said Spike. "I think I'll take my flippers," he added.

They pulled on their knapsacks—oh, they were heavy!—and set off for their picnic.

"Let's not stop until we get to the pond," said Little Willy.

"I'm starving already," groaned Spike.

On they trudged. Their packs grew heavier with every step. They stumbled through the high grass and under the wild apple

tree. And then...

    "Here we are!" cried Little Willy.

    "At last!" sighed Spike, happily.

    They were both starving.

    "And now for the picnic!" said Little Willy with a grin.

    "I've been dreaming of a sandwich," said Spike. He reached into his knapsack. "But where *are* they?"

    "Maybe I have them," said Little Willy. He reached into his knapsack. "Oh, no!" he cried.

    "What?"

    "Spike, I forgot my picnic!" said Little Willy.

    "I forgot mine, too!" said Spike mournfully.

    "Oooooh!" groaned the pair of them.

"Our picnic is sitting on the kitchen table," said Little Willy gloomily.

"And after all that work," moaned Spike.

"I've never been so hungry in all my life," said Little Willy.

"Or so miserable," said Spike.

"Remember all the peanut butter sandwiches I made?" asked Little Willy.

"And the chocolate cake. And the apples. And the cookies. And the lemonade!" cried Spike.

"Ooooh!" they howled.

"And to think we carried all these heavy things with us. Now I'm much too hungry to play!"

"Oooooooh!"

Just then the tall grass parted and there was the friendly face of Owley.

"Hello!" said Spike. "You were lucky you couldn't come to the picnic."

"We forgot the *food!*" cried Little Willy.

"I know," said Owley.

"You do?"

"Yes. I finished my chores early. So I went to your house. And your mother put the picnic in the wagon," he said.

"She did?" asked Little Willy.

"Yes. Look, it's right here."

And it was.

They all sat down together. They just couldn't wait to begin.

"Now isn't it lucky that we packed too much food?" asked Spike.

He handed the first sandwich to Owley, who deserved it.

"We had too many sandwiches. Too many cookies," said Spike.

"But it's going to be just enough!" said Owley happily.

The Haunted House

Spike had stayed at Little Willy's house for supper.

"I think it's time for you to go home now, dear," said Mrs. Rabbit.

Spike looked down at the floor and said, "Could Little Willy walk me home, Mrs. Rabbit?"

"Why, Spike, are you afraid to walk through the woods at night?" she asked.

"Yes, ma'am," replied Spike.

"Me, too," piped in Little Willy.

"Well, whatever has happened? You were never afraid before," she said.

"It's because of the haunted house," said Little Willy.

"There is no such thing!" said Mrs. Rabbit, laughing.

"Oh, yes, there is!" cried Spike. "It's the fourth pine tree from the pond. It's haunted!"

"Strange noises come out of it. And a light flickers inside," whispered Little Willy. A shiver of fright shook him all over.

"Well, never mind, Spike. Little Willy will walk home with you," said Mother Rabbit.

"Do I have to, Mom?" asked Little Willy in a squeaky voice.

"Yes!" said his mother firmly. "A haunted house! That's silly!"

The two friends opened the door into the black night. And they jumped at every soft rustle in the grass.

As they neared the spooky pine tree they tiptoed. They hoped they could run past it. Then...

"Listen," whispered Little Willy.

There was a scraping sound inside the tree trunk.

"Oooh, I'm scared!" wailed Spike.

"Shh!" hissed Little Willy.

Suddenly a light flickered inside the tree.

Then a face peered out, lit by a candle.

A voice whispered, "Who's there?"

Little Willy and Spike were too frightened to speak.

"Why don't you answer?" cried the voice.

The candle's light reached into the darkness and they could see who was there.

"Why, Raccoon, it's you!" cried Little Willy.

"Is that you, Little Willy and Spike? Oh, you gave me such a fright!" called Raccoon.

"We thought this was a haunted house!" Little Willy exclaimed.

"No. Come inside and you'll see," said Raccoon with a laugh.

Well, inside the hollow tree Raccoon was making a house for himself. And, oddly, everything looked familiar.

"Raccoon, isn't that my father's old chair that Mother threw out last week?" asked Little Willy.

"Could be," said Raccoon.

"And that table is the one we used for a raft one time," said Spike.

"Maybe," said Raccoon.

He offered them some stale cookies, baked by Mother Rabbit three days ago, on her cracked, blue plate.

Mmmm. They still tasted pretty good.

"I just pick up things that are left outside by the trash bin," said Raccoon. "It's nice to live with things that once belonged to friends."

"It will be a nice, cozy house very soon," said Little Willy.

"We're glad you're not a haunted house!" said Spike, and he looked around nervously.

"Come again soon!" called Raccoon from the tree.

"Good night!" called his friends.

Little Willy and Spike were not one bit afraid as they ran home in the night.

And both of them could think of some little things, in the cellar and the attic, that Raccoon could use. With a bit of help, he'd have a real home in no time!

The Birthday Party

"Happy birthday, Little Willy," said Mother Rabbit. And she gave him a kiss.

Little Willy was so excited that he couldn't eat his breakfast.

"Today I am having a birthday party. My very first!" he cried.

He was so excited that he jumped up from his chair and danced around the room.

"When will the party be?" he asked.

"In a little while. Now you go and get washed. And, Little Willy…"

"Yes, Mommy?"

"Don't come into the kitchen for a while," Mother said.

"I won't."

In just a few minutes he asked through the keyhole, "Is it time for the party, Mommy?"

"No, Little Willy. You go off for a nice birthday walk."

Little Willy took a very quick little walk to the rosebush and back.

"I had my birthday walk, Mommy. Is it time for the party?" he called up through the kitchen window.

"Not yet, Little Willy. Go and see how many cartwheels you can do on your birthday," Mother suggested.

"It's me again," Little Willy soon said.

"I thought so," answered Mother.

"I did three cartwheels."

"You are growing up," said Mother, through the door.

"I don't think I can wait any longer, Mom!" he exclaimed.

Just then, his friends arrived, calling, "Happy birthday, Little Willy!"

Oh, he was so pleased. There were Spike and Owley and Raccoon.

"Mommy, they are here! It's time for my birthday party!" cried Little Willy.

"It is time," said Mother. And she opened the door wide.

Little Willy could hardly believe his eyes. Hanging over the big table was a huge bouquet of balloons. On the wall was a paper donkey. And on the table were lots of birthday presents.

"Everything is so pretty!" said Little Willy. "Can I open my presents now?"

"Not yet," said Mother. "We're going to play the games first."

They played Pin the Tail on the Donkey.

Spike won the prize. It was a harmonica. He loved it.

Raccoon won the game of musical chairs. He got soap bubbles.

Then Mother called everyone to the table.

"Could I please open my presents now?" asked Little Willy.

"Yes, dear, you may," Mother said.

AT LAST!

Little Willy was so excited as he pulled the ribbon on the first one. It was from Spike. A little wooden boat.

"Oh, thank you, Spike!" Little Willy said.

Owley couldn't wait for his present to be opened.

"You'll never guess what it is," he said. "It's a ba—"

"*Shhhh!*" Everyone shushed him as Little Willy opened the big, round package. It was a red ball. And it bounced, bounced right into a corner.

"Thank you, Owley. We'll really use that ball," said Little Willy.

Raccoon gave him a paddle with a ball attached. Little Willy tried it out right away.

Bang! It hit Spike in the head. But it didn't hurt.

From Mother and Daddy there was a boomerang. And some roller skates.

Oh, Little Willy was so happy.

"And now...something is going to happen," said Owley.

Everyone began to sing "Happy Birthday, Little Willy!" And Mother came to the table with the most beautiful cake. There seemed to be a hundred candles glowing on it.

"It's beautiful, Mommy," said Little Willy.

"Now you must make a wish and blow out all the candles. Then your wish will come true," said Mother.

"What can I wish?" asked Little Willy.

"Quick! The candles are melting," cried Spike. Little Willy was too happy to wish for anything.

"Hurry!" cried Raccoon.

"Oh, I know what I can wish!" cried Little Willy.

He closed his eyes and blew. When he opened them, all the candles were out. And everybody cheered.

"Your wish will come true," said Mother.

That made him so happy. Because his secret wish was, "I hope that my next birthday will be just like this one!"

It's More Fun
When You Know

Little Willy and Spike were swimming in the pond. With his swimming mask on his face, Little Willy was exploring the plants growing under the water.

Every few minutes he would pop up for air and tell Spike about the wonderful things he had seen.

"You ought to get a mask, Spike. Here, try mine. Go ahead and look!" cried Little Willy.

"I don't like to put my face under water," said Spike.

"But you wouldn't believe what's down there!" said Little Willy.

"That's the whole thing! I don't want to see what's down there. Octopuses! Sharks! Crabs!" Spike shuddered and paddled close to Little Willy's side for company.

"That's silly. There aren't any sharks in a pond. Or octopuses," said Little Willy.

"Just thinking about them makes me scared."

Spike paddled close to Little Willy to take hold of his arm.

"Is that you I'm touching?" he asked.

"Yes," giggled his friend. And he ducked under the water again.

Spike turned on his back and floated. He wished that he hadn't said the words *shark* or *octopuses* or even *crab*.

He was thinking about these things when suddenly his foot touched something....

"Eeeeek!" He collapsed under the water in a cloud of bubbles. Then he came up again, spluttering, and paddled to shore as fast as he could go.

Little Willy bobbed up from exploring the underwater garden. "Where are you going?" he called.

Spike flung himself on the grassy bank, panting.

"I t-touched something. I think it wanted to bite me," he gasped.

"The reason you're scared is because you don't know what's down there," said Little Willy.

"I'm not scared!" said Spike.

"Then put on this mask and duck under," said Little Willy.

"O.K. Just to prove I'm not a scaredy-cat," said Spike.

Gingerly, he put the face mask over his head. Then he pulled it off again.

50

"Not that way. Here, I'll show you."

And, gently, Little Willy coaxed Spike to put the mask on and then his head under water.

Right away Spike bobbed up again.

"I—I ha a hish dat bid!" he cried.

He pulled off the mask and said, "I saw a fish that big. Huge!" And he pulled the mask on again.

"You'll see lots of them!" Little Willy said, happily.

They paddled around with their heads underwater for awhile.

Spike popped up for air and said, "It's pretty the way the plants wave in the water!"

"Didn't I tell you?" cried Little Willy.

After a long swim together they waded to shore and lay on the grass to get warm.

"That was terrific! I'm going to ask my mother for a mask of my very own," said Spike.

"Good. And I don't think you'll ever feel nervous in the water again," said Little Willy.

"Not now. Because I know what's down there. It's really pretty!" said Spike.

51

The Train

"Chuff-chuff-chuff!"

"Chuff-chuff-chuff!"

Little Willy and Spike ran across the front lawn pumping their arms and legs up and down. Between them they held a rope. And tied to Little Willy's head was a tall roll of cardboard.

"Ding! Ding! Ding! Ding!" called Little Willy and Spike.

Then into the garden came Owley.

"Be careful, Owley. You're standing on the track," called Little Willy.

"What track?" asked Owley.

"The train track," said Spike. "Can't you see we're a train?"

"Not really," said Owley.

The train stopped chuffing.

"Don't we LOOK like a train?" asked Little Willy.

"No," said Owley.

"I'm the engine. See this thing on my head? That's the smokestack," explained Little Willy.

"And I'm the caboose that the engine is pulling. Doesn't everybody know we're being a train?"

"I don't think so," said Owley.

"Well, you almost got run over on the track," said Little Willy.

"Thank you for stopping," said Owley.

Little Willy sat down on the grass and sighed.

"I wish we had a nice, long train with lots of passenger cars," he said.

"Me, too," said Spike.

He looked around the garden, but there was nothing that looked like passenger cars.

"Little Willy, your mother is calling you," said Owley. And she was.

"Hoo! Hoo!" called Mother Rabbit. "Could you take these cardboard boxes and put them somewhere until Daddy can take them away?"

"Yes, Mommy," said Little Willy.

And, just for fun, he put one box on top of his head as he carried it off the porch.

Spike put a box on his head, too.

And so did Owley.

They walked around for a while like that. Then they bumped into each other, and sat down, laughing.

The boxes tumbled on the grass and lay there, in a row.

They landed in such a nice, neat row, one behind the other. The three friends looked at each other and grinned. They all had the same idea at once.

Little Willy ran for the crayons.

"And bring some scissors!" called Spike.

There, on the grass, they made passenger cars out of the cardboard boxes. They drew wheels on the sides of the boxes. In front they drew big lamps. And on the tops they cut holes to put their heads through.

What a nice, long passenger train they made!

"Chuff! Chuff! Chuff! Chuff! Chuff! Chuff!"

Off across the grass they went, huffing and chuffing the whole morning. And then it was time to fill up the tank with some tuna fish sandwiches.

Father Rabbit's Good Idea

When Little Willy went to bed at night all his dolls went with him. He loved them all. He said good night to every one.

There were so many people in Little Willy's bed that sometimes one of them fell on the floor.

Thump!

Oh, dear. When he climbed out of bed to rescue his friend, everyone else tumbled out, too.

So they all had to be tucked in once more.

One night, Little Willy bent over to cover up Bear, and out of the bed fell Brownie the Dog.

Thump!

Little Willy climbed patiently down from the bed for Brownie, when out onto the floor tumbled Teddy and Lion.

Thump! Thump!

"What are we going to do?" asked Little Willy, holding his family in his arms.

Then he had an idea.

He would sleep on the carpet with Teddy. The rest of the dolls
would have his bed.

Nobody looked very happy. But what could he do?

He tried to sleep on the carpet. He turned on his back. Then he
turned on his front. He was cold. There was no blanket.

Suddenly the door opened. Daddy was coming in to say good
night.

"Well, what is this, Little Willy? Have your friends pushed
you out of bed?" asked Father.

"There are just too many of us, Daddy," said Little Willy.
"I have given them my bed."

"They could sleep in the toybox," said Father.

"But they are used to sleeping in a soft bed," said Little Willy.

Father went to the closet, and came back carrying a pillow.

"I think I have the answer," he said.

He pulled the blanket and sheet from the foot of the bed. Then he put the pillow there.

"Oh, Daddy, that's wonderful," said Little Willy.

It was hard, of course, to choose who would sleep at the bottom of the bed and who would sleep at the top, with Little Willy.

"They can take turns," said Father.

Little Willy climbed back into bed and leaned against the pillow.

What a lot of room he had! And it was fun to look down at the foot of the bed and see his friends. He waved.

Then suddenly he disappeared. Under the cover a little shape moved down to the end of the bed. Then he popped up on the pillow at the foot of his bed.

"*I* can take turns, too!" he laughed.

Now, didn't Father Rabbit have a good idea?

The New Pet

Late one night a strange noise came from Little Willy's room.

Thump! Thump! Thump!

His mother opened Little Willy's door.

"Eeek!" she squeaked, as something small hopped under the bed.

"Close the door, Mommy. He might escape!" cried Little Willy. Then he scrambled under the bed.

"What is it? What is it?" gasped Mother. She leaped on a stool and clutched her nightgown around her.

There were more scuffles from under the bed.

"It's my new pet, Mommy. He's cute," said Little Willy.

"Wh-what kind of a pet is it?" asked Mother, nervously.

"He's...oh! There he goes again. Look out!" cried Little Willy.

"Eeeek!" squeaked Mother Rabbit.

"Here he comes!" shouted Little Willy.

The new pet leaped on to the bed and made a dash for the windowsill, where it hid behind the curtain.

Little Willy made a lunge for the curtain.

"Got him!" He squealed with delight. And he held up the new pet for Mother to see.

"There, isn't he cute? His name is Freddy," said Little Willy.

Just then the door was flung open. And there was Father Rabbit, half asleep.

"Do you know what time it is?" he thundered. "What is going on?"

"Meet my new pet, Daddy. His name is Freddy. Freddy Frog. Isn't he cute?"

He held up his pet and the frog croaked.

"I think that frog should go home and let us get some sleep," said Father Rabbit.

The frog croaked again.

"But he's my pet. I caught him," wailed Little Willy.

"Put him out the window," said Father.

"But Daddy, he loves me," pleaded Little Willy, clinging to the wriggling frog. It croaked once again.

"He will love you more if you let him go home to his mother," said Father Rabbit.

The frog croaked loudly.

"See? He is saying he doesn't want to go!" said Little Willy.

"Then tell him he MUST go, because your father needs his sleep!" Father Rabbit's voice rose dangerously.

Slowly, Little Willy carried his new pet to the window. He gave it a kiss, then he let it go.

The frog hopped from the windowsill to the grass. He hopped away in the moonlight.

Little Willy watched him sadly. Then suddenly he cried, "LOOK!"

They all looked outside, and there was the little frog waving good-by in the moonlight.

"Bye-bye, Freddy," called Little Willy. "I'll come to visit you at the pond!"

"There. Now he really loves you because you let him go," said Mother.

"Good old Freddy," said Father Rabbit, as he padded back to his bed.